P9-BYS-903

# Daredevil Club

## Pam Withers

ORCA BOOK PUBLISHERS

**Library and Archives Canada Cataloguing in Publication**

Withers, Pam

Daredevil Club / Pam Withers.

(Orca currents)

ISBN 1-55143-618-3 (bound) 1-55143-614-0 (pbk.)

I. Title. II. Series.

PS8613.R367P53 2006      iC813'.6      C2006-903444-3

**Summary:** Kip struggles to maintain his status as a daredevil
in spite of his disability.

First published in the United States, 2006
**Library of Congress Control Number:** 2006928965

Orca Book Publishers gratefully acknowledges the support for its publishing
programs provided by the following agencies: the Government of Canada
through the Book Publishing Industry Development Program and the
Canada Council for the Arts, and the Province of British Columbia
through the BC Arts Council and the Book Publishing Tax Credit.

Cover design: Lynn O'Rourke
Cover photography: Getty Images

Orca Book Publishers                    Orca Book Publishers
PO Box 5626, Station B                  PO Box 468
Victoria, BC Canada                     Custer, WA USA
V8R 6S4                                 98240-0468

www.orcabook.com
Printed and bound in Canada

09  08 07  06  •  4  3  2  1

Other books by Pam Withers

*Breathless*
*Camp Wild*

# chapter one

Climbing the old water tower was number five on our list. We chose to do it during a downpour. Not just 'cause the cops were onto us after our first four stunts. They'd almost caught us on number three.

The fear of getting caught was part of the excitement. The police in our little town, assuming they'd heard rumors of our "seven dares," had to be waiting for us to tackle the old tower on the hill at some point. We'd also chosen a dark and stormy night 'cause the tower was dry inside. Our town's water tower is shaped like a giant toilet-paper roll wearing a funnel cap. We figured since it had a roof, the tower should be dry inside. That meant the ladder running up the inside wall shouldn't be too rotten.

We couldn't know for sure, because no one had been inside the tower for years, not since the town had declared it an "impure" source of water and boarded it up. All the place was good for was being broken into. And who better to grab the honors than the Daredevil Club? Besides, what else was there to do during a rainstorm?

A hundred yards from the tower, Fraser, Vlad, Caleb and I dropped to our stomachs and slithered through the mud under the barbed-wire fence. Did the townsfolk of Peever really think a mere barbed-wire fence would stop the mighty members of the Daredevil Club? Not even our competitors, the Wildmen, would pause for a barbed-wire fence.

"Shoot," I muttered as the back of my rain jacket caught on a barb.

"I've got it," Caleb said, reaching down and freeing me. Then he grabbed my hands, pulled me through the last few feet, and handed me my cane. For someone half a head shorter than me, Caleb is pretty strong. Too bad he's not as gutsy as he is strong. He only got into the club 'cause I recommended him, and he knows it.

"Don't need your help," I protested as I sat up. I used my finger to take a layer of mud off my cane. I wiped the fingerful of slime on the fencepost. Then I shoved my cane deep into the mud and leaned on it to rise. Caleb knew not to reach out to help me.

"Hold on, guys," he was calling softly to the others. "Wait for Kip." They were halfway to the tower. They were visible only by the pricks of light from their flashlights.

"We'll catch them," I said, lifting my left foot into place with my hands and aiming it toward the tower. I didn't expect the guys to wait up for me. I had to prove I could keep up. It was part of tonight's test: the test to see if I could stay in the Daredevil Club after my accident.

"Stop hovering," I commanded Caleb. He was annoying me. Maybe I was just grumpy from the shot of pain that came with trying to put myself back into motion. I had to move faster, or I was a sitting duck for the police. The guys knew that. It was amazing they had even let me come along on number five. But I'd insisted, and I'm pretty strong-willed. Plus, the whole club had been my idea. Fraser and Vlad had just enough guilt about the accident that they wouldn't keep me from trying at least one more stunt.

I also knew that if anyone chased us, Fraser and Vlad would disappear. Only Caleb would stick around to keep an eye out for his gimpy friend. That was an unspoken part of the deal: a rotten deal that stemmed from rotten luck on stunt number four. But I started this club. I helped build the list of seven dares. And I was going to finish it with the team. Even if Fraser had taken over as the leader.

I'd already coped with months of pain and torturous physio exercises. I also knew my friends weren't okay about the accident. Sure, they came to my house at first. My overly cheerful mom would lead them into my bedroom, where I lay with my leg elevated. They'd glance nervously at the pain pills cluttering my bedside table. Then they'd sit on the edge of chairs that my mom dragged in, their eyes darting out the window. They'd try hard to make small talk. Pretty soon we'd run out of stuff to say. Then they'd rise and punch me gently and say—quietly so my mom wouldn't hear—"Can't wait till it's all mended, dude, so we can finish the dares."

Every day I feared they'd say, "Dude, we can't wait anymore. We're going to finish those dares without you, okay?" Trying to keep that from happening was everything that drove me after the accident.

By the time Caleb and I reached the water tower's door, Fraser and Vlad had tugged its wet boards off with their crowbars. The inside of the tower was dark and smelled like rotten eggs and mold. I scrunched up my nose.

"Good place to shoot a horror movie," Fraser muttered.

"Get a load of the pigeon droppings," Vlad said, kicking piles of white muck, then coughing. I didn't bother telling them that it was poisonous.

Four flashlight beams arced around the place. Fraser's beam raced along walls weeping with humidity.

"Black as tar," Vlad said. He reached out to touch the black and withdrew his hand quickly.

"Weird. It's loose like coffee grounds."

"Cockroach droppings," I informed them, prompting Vlad to wipe his hands vigorously against a pant leg.

One by one, we raised our flashlight beams to the underside of the roof. It was dark. But even in the dim light, we could see that the darkness was moving. It undulated like "the wave" at a hockey game. The cockroaches protested our entry by releasing their hold on the ceiling and flying down at us.

"I'm outta here," Caleb said, heading for the doorway.

"Not so fast," I said, my fingers closing tightly on his collar. "Pull your hood up, Caleb, and get on that ladder. I'll go last."

I hoped that last sentence didn't sound too bitter. I also hoped that all the weights I'd been pumping would help me haul my nonworking leg up. I gripped the ladder beneath my three buddies and hung my cane on one of the lower rungs.

My breathing was heavy, my hands were sweaty. But with one pull after another, I kept climbing.

"Keep your eyes and mouth shut," Fraser called down. "The cockroaches are epic up here."

Caleb threw me an alarmed glance, but he knew I blocked his retreat.

Wimp, I thought. And he has four operating limbs. I set my jaw and kept going. The others were waiting when I reached the top. Fraser and Vlad tried to mask their impatience. Caleb was too distracted by the battery of bugs and protesting pigeons to address me. I got no slap on the back or words of encouragement. You'd hardly know I used to be leader of this group. They either had no idea what a feat the climb had been for me, or they were only tolerating my presence.

I started down with no rest. I'd made it. Did that mean they'd let me do the next two? If I could do this, I could probably do the drainpipe crawl, number six, and the abandoned grain elevator just outside town, our number seven. There was no going back to the guy I had been three months earlier. But surely, I hoped, it was enough that they'd held off doing number five until I'd mended enough to come along. Hanging from one rotten rung after another, dangling my useless leg beside my working foot, I descended as fast as I dared. Pigeons' wings fanned my face, rain pounded the thin walls of the tower, and cockroaches dive-bombed my ears. Three pairs of feet above me adopted a stop-and-go descent to accommodate me.

Silently I told myself, "They're impressed, and I'm still in the club."

## chapter two

"Kip Fox! What's the meaning of the muddy clothes?" my mom demanded from my bedroom doorway.

I blinked awake.

"Well? I'm waiting," she said. A sock encrusted with dried mud dangled from her fingertips.

"Uh, sorry Mom. I slipped on my way home from Caleb's last night."

"Slipped?" She waved the sock like it was a checkered flag at the finish line of a car race. "More like *rolled* in mud. What would you be doing that would have you rolling in mud?"

"Mom, I told you, I slipped. Can I go back to sleep now?" I rearranged the pillow under my head.

She crossed her arms and squinted at me. "You weren't out doing any silly stunts last night, were you?" The tone was softer now. It held a slight tremor.

I produced a dramatic sigh. "Mom, I told you, I slipped. Stop worrying."

"Did you hurt yourself?" Now she was staring at the outline of my legs under the quilt. She moved farther into the room and perched on the edge of my bed. "Your father and I..." she began.

I braced.

"We just want to feel certain that, given all you've been through the last few months— all that the *entire family* has gone through as a result of your last shenanigan..."

"Mom, leave it," I said, pulling my pillow over my ears. "I'll deal with those clothes when I get up, okay?"

11

She didn't leave right away. She sat there, hands fidgeting with the sock, eyes traveling around my room. They rested on my hockey trophies, souvenirs of a past life, a past city. There was no hockey rink in this hick town. In Peever, there wasn't much to do at all. Or many people to do it with. Her eyes moved to my cane. She attempted a smile and rested a hand on my head.

"Sorry, dear. We just want to feel certain that you learned a lesson. I don't like worrying about you every time you go out. Ever since we moved here, you seem to be…" Her voice trailed off.

"Seem to be what, Mom?" My own voice had a warning in it.

"To be asking for trouble. You seem to have lost your common sense."

She paused. I could feel a vein pulsing in my forehead. "*Mom.*"

"I never used to worry, you know. But your new friends here—I worry sometimes they're a bad influence. They're so different from the type of boys you used to hang out with in…"

"Mom! You and Dad were the ones that made us move. It's not like there are many kids to choose from here! And there's nothing wrong with my friends anyway!"

Her eyes moved to the sock in her hand, and she took the hint to lay off the lame lecture. Ha! I thought. She has no idea I was the one who came up with the list of stunts in the first place. She also has no idea that Fraser, Vlad, Caleb, and I got away with several great ones before my accident.

For number one we jumped from branch to branch high up in three-story-tall trees in a grove near the school. Number two was a downhill shopping-cart race. Number three was bungee jumping, number four was a jump off a cliff into a lake. Some kids at school regard us as heroes; we've gotten a ton of attention. Why else would the Wildmen have started copying us?

I grinned inwardly. Fraser and Vlad a bad influence on me? Not likely. But parents need to be kept clueless. They worry too much. Especially mine.

I suppose my accident did put them through the wringer.

"Sorry, dear," Mom said. "Would you like some pancakes for breakfast?"

"If I'm not allowed to go back to sleep," I grumbled, reaching for my cane.

Caleb showed up mid-day. He found me up to my elbows in laundry soap at the kitchen sink.

"Hello, Caleb," my father greeted him, peering over the top of his newspaper. "You boys have fun last night?"

Caleb shot a glance in my direction, then stole a look at my mother, who was watching him closely. "Uh, yeah. Good video at my house."

"Really? What did you watch?" my mother was quick to ask.

Caleb studied the suds that had spilled over the sink and were sliding down my cane. "*Haunted Tower*, or something like that."

"Sounds like a horror flick. Used to like those myself," my father said, newspaper crinkling as he turned a page. "You boys off somewhere today? Your mother and I would like to know exactly where you're going. Otherwise we worry," he added, looking directly at me.

"Cowboy Café for lunch," Caleb replied before I could.

"Safe enough for you, Dad?" I asked as I pulled the stopper in the sink.

"Thanks, Kip. I'll take care of them from here," my mother said, moving toward me with a laundry basket. "See you after lunch, then, boys."

"Cowboy Café for lunch?" I questioned Caleb as we got out the door. "What gives?"

"We're meeting Fraser and Vlad there. The Wildmen heard about us last night." His voice was low as we passed some neighbors.

I smiled. "Good!"

He frowned and bit a thumbnail. "Trouble is, they got up to one of their own last night."

"Ah. That would be their number four. We're still one ahead. What was it?"

"The grain elevator," Caleb said.

I mirrored his frown. "Shoot. So they've

gone and done our number seven. The posers."

"Fraser and Vlad are pretty choked. Wonder what they'll decide we do about it?"

I winced at how Caleb expected Fraser and Vlad to dictate what we do next, not me. Then again, why would a cripple lead a stunt team? I paused and stood tall, my cane behind my back for a second. "I have an idea for a new number seven that'll blow the Wildmen's socks off."

Caleb grinned.

Ten minutes later, I was explaining it to Fraser and Vlad. "So we pull ourselves along the steel girders that support the old highway bridge, all the way to the other side of the lake. The big trick will be not falling on the rocks beneath the bridge, where the bank drops away, before we're over the water."

"Or preferably not falling at all," Fraser replied sternly, stroking his chin. Vlad sat beside Fraser, arms crossed, pretending he wasn't impressed with the idea. Caleb was looking from one to the other, excited but clearly hesitant to show it.

After a minute, Vlad plunged a French fry into the pool of ketchup on his plate. "The bridge sounds okay to me."

Fraser opened his burger's bun and studied it like a food inspector. Finally he picked it up and sank his teeth into it. "Bridge could be doable," he agreed with his mouth full.

They're jealous that I thought of it first, I decided.

"It's a great idea!" Caleb inserted, but piped down when the other two sent him withering looks.

"Sure you're up for it?" Fraser said, turning so that his eyes were on my cane.

"Kip wouldn't have suggested it if he couldn't do it," Caleb jumped in.

"Sure *you're* up for it?" I responded evenly to Fraser.

# chapter three

I hated the way the bells jingled whenever the door of the physiotherapist's office opened. The noise mocked my efforts at holding the door open with my cane while I dragged my left foot in.

For me those jingling bells delivered the less-than-cheery message, "For the next hour, you will experience excruciating pain. Then you'll go home and collapse."

Well, I *had* gotten better, hadn't I? I'd gone from not being able to walk, to being able to shuffle. Never mind that I had to carry a cane like an old man. What would I give to be done with physiotherapy? To never set foot in this clinic again? Or better yet, to never have come here in the first place?

I didn't buy the argument that I'd asked for trouble that day. I hadn't taken a big risk. All the other boys had jumped off the cliff and dropped into the water cleanly. I was the only one who'd dropped onto the underwater rock and smashed my leg to bits. It was a freak accident. A number four that none of us would ever forget.

"Kip! Right on time as always," Andrew Pollack, my physio, greeted me. He was wearing a black T-shirt and jeans. He was young and played bass in a rock band. He was okay, Andrew. He seemed to know what it took to get broken parts moving again. Rumor had it he'd taken this job for very little money, because he liked the community. Why anyone would *voluntarily* move to Peever was beyond me, but I was glad he had. If not for him, I'd probably still be in a wheelchair. When I'd first started here, the exercises had nearly killed me. Like running marathons daily with knives buried in your hip and leg. Andrew had coached me through the blur of pain. He'd kept me at it when I was on the brink of quitting. He never offered sympathy, just encouragement. He never let anyone do less than he felt they were capable of doing.

"Come on through," he continued. "I'll introduce you to our new volunteer. She's on a work-experience program."

Just what I need, I thought. Someone to observe me in the torture chamber.

The minute we entered the workout room, I wanted to leave. I recognized her, all right: Elyse Strauss. A pain in the neck who went to my school. Age thirteen. Totally unathletic. Little Miss Know-It-All. Student council fundraising person, chess club star, and secretary of our school's recycling committee.

As far as I was concerned, *she* should be recycled. The first time I met Elyse, she just walked up and started yelling at me.

"What kind of idiots would race shopping carts down a hill?" she'd demanded, hands on her hips like she was a teacher. "You're going to get Caleb injured. Why don't you act your age?"

Caleb was her cousin.

"Racing shopping carts?" I'd said. "Total idiocy, I agree. Me, I'm thinking about joining the chess club. I hear it really works your biceps."

That had made her sputter, spin, and march down the hall. It sure had gotten everyone around me laughing too. Not many people liked Elyse Strauss.

And now here she was about to witness the consequences of my stunts. Great.

"Kip," Andrew was saying, "this is Elyse. She wants to be a doctor, and her summer work-experience program has arranged for her to help out here. Elyse, this is Kip."

Awkward silence reigned as I glared at her, and she shifted from one polished shoe to another. As a volunteer she had to look professional in front of Andrew. She extended her hand.

"Kip, good to see you. Mr. Pollack refers to you as his star patient. I guess that means many people can learn from your example."

Her sneer was so subtle that Andrew probably didn't catch it—or the double meaning.

"Elyse Strauss," I said as smoothly as I could, lifting my cane to point it at her so that she had to back up an inch. "From chess club, which I keep meaning to join."

She reddened only slightly.

"So you know each other. That's good," Andrew said, clipping pages onto his clipboard. "Kip, let's see if your workouts have increased your range of movement this week. I'm hoping for big things today."

That meant big pain, I knew. But I knew I could handle it. I had to handle it. I was an athlete. I was competitive. Just because I wasn't in sports anymore didn't mean I lacked an opponent. My adversary was the part of me that still didn't work.

"Elyse, why don't you fetch the ball," Andrew directed his student helper.

Go Spot, go. Fetch the ball, I wanted to say.

Andrew directed me to lie down on the gym mat and put my legs up and over the big rubber ball. Getting my good leg up there was easy. Have you ever tried moving a mostly lifeless, rubber-like appendage up onto a slippery, rolling surface? Elyse hung back and watched. I froze my face into a mask that reflected no pain. Within seconds we were into the whole routine. I did the core body exercises. I lifted weights. I activated muscles where muscles didn't know they were supposed to be. I moved body parts that were still relearning they were body parts. And I worked extra hard not to grimace or cry out. I hated that Elyse was there. I knew she was thinking I'd brought this on myself.

I stopped, totally spent, after my final exercise: twenty-five chin-ups. Chin-ups weren't a big deal before my enforced three months of bed rest. But my accident had not only knocked out my lower body strength; it had also forced me to start from scratch with my upper body strength.

"I'd say you have three more of those in you," Andrew declared.

"You think?" I said tiredly. I tried. I really tried, but I couldn't pull myself up again.

"Put your mind into it, not just your body. Think of a reason you have to do three more, Kip."

I closed my eyes. I visualized the steel girders on the highway bridge. I managed one more. When the next one failed me, I pictured Fraser, Vlad, and Caleb reaching the far side of the bridge with victory smiles as I clung to the cold metal in the middle of the bridge. For the final chin-up, I pictured Fraser and Vlad exchanging a decisive *look*.

"Excellent, Kip. Knew you could do it. Take a breather. Now look at this chart." He squatted down beside me as I wiped sweat off my forehead and accepted the cup of water Elyse offered. "Just three months ago, you'd lost most of your upper and lower body strength, and couldn't move your left leg at all."

"I remember," I said. I watched an elderly man wander in. He nodded at Andrew and accepted Elyse's hand to help him over to the stationary bikes. But she was looking back at us, trying to hear what we said.

"Now you're bench-pressing twenty percent more than you did when you were playing hockey."

"And starting to get some response from the injured leg," I finished for him.

"I predict you'll be finished with me in another few months," Andrew said, lowering the chart and patting my totally juiced arms. He seemed prouder than a new dad, and I couldn't help but feel pleased with myself.

"I appreciate it, coach," I said.

"It's not me that has done it, Kip. You're my most motivated patient. I'm not sure what's driving you, but I wish I could bottle it for the rest of my patients."

I smiled and leveled a look at Elyse.

"You bottle what he's got," she said, "and you'll need to label it with a skull and crossbones."

Andrew was still scratching his head as I exited the clinic.

## chapter four

"Looks like it might rain pretty hard," I said to Fraser as we trudged up the dirt road toward Peever's biggest hill. I eyed black thunderclouds moving in from the east. I smelled dust embracing the droplets. I wondered what exactly the weather had in store.

"That'll make it more exciting," Fraser replied between long strides. His rain pants swished as he walked.

"Yeah, it could make for a flash flood. Whoooosh!" Vlad suggested, waving his arms about as water dripped off the bill of his backward baseball cap down the back of his raincoat.

"But if it starts raining really hard, shouldn't we do it another day?" Caleb was trying to sound very casual. His new rubber boots squeaked with each footstep.

"And let the Wildmen beat us out?" Fraser demanded angrily. "They could be doing their number five right now!"

"The faster we move, the less trouble the rain will make for us," I reminded them, swinging my cane so efficiently that I pulled ahead of all three. I'd caught sight of where the steel culvert—the tunnel-size drainpipe—emerged from the hillside.

We stopped either side of the culvert and peered in. Muddy water was flowing out, maybe only two inches deep. Still, the current was strong enough to move pebbles over the lip. I flicked on my flashlight and peered in. The corrugated steel tunnel was too low to walk through. We'd have to crawl on our knees. Or in my case, my knee. Good thing I'd brought a backpack to stuff my cane into.

We knew where the culvert started: the other side of the hill, below a waterfall-fed stream. We just didn't know how many twists and turns it took between here and there. We didn't know if mud and stones blocked it in places. That, of course, is what made it exciting. It's what had earned it number six status. We'd be the first people to crawl through the entire thing.

"Probably has rats in it," Vlad said to Caleb with a smirk directed at Fraser.

"I doubt it," Caleb returned bravely, his face a little white.

"And spiders," Fraser added jovially as he pulled up his sweatshirt hood and fixed a headlamp around it.

"Spiders are better than cockroaches," Caleb retorted. "Besides, any spiders in here would be drowned. The water flow is picking up already."

"Of course it is," Vlad declared. "It's raining, isn't it? We'd better get a move on.

It isn't supposed to be a swimming stunt."

I pulled on my bike gloves. The trickle was becoming a hurried stream. I adjusted the hockey knee pads I'd slipped on under my trousers.

"I'm going first," I announced, getting down on all fours and tucking my cane into the straps on my backpack.

"Says who?" Fraser demanded.

"We need to stick close together. I'll set the pace," I said. If I went last, they'd get so far ahead that no one would be able to help me if I got into trouble. Besides, I'd been bench-pressing major weights. And I had the knee pad advantage.

Sloshing through wrist-high flowing water was no fun. Hitting sharp rocks and unexpected piles of stuck-together mud and stones beneath the water was no fun. Crawling in the dark not knowing when a rat might splash beneath you was no fun. And feeling spider webs against my face gave me the shivers.

The unevenness of the corrugated steel stubbed my fingers right through my gloves.

My nostrils took in the damp. I lifted my nose to sniff like a dog and felt the air blowing past me. That was a good thing, because it meant a clear tunnel, right?

I turned my head around after ten minutes. "Everyone okay?" My voice sounded muffled. Then I heard my muffled echo. Cool. Like being in a cave. But a very tight cave.

"We're fine," came the response.

There was room to twist my head, but none to turn my body around. If anything halted us, we'd be backing out. Wouldn't that be fun? Then again, if the stream now up to my elbows kept rising, maybe we'd be *flushed* out backward.

My outstretched hands slapped the water as they pulled me forward. My good knee pushed off the culvert's bottom, or off whatever debris had collected in small piles. The water filling my boots chilled me. The good knee worked with my stomach muscles to drag my left leg along. Slap, slap, push, drag. I was proud of how far my workouts had taken me. I couldn't have done this without them. Slap, slap, push, drag. I had a great rhythm going. In fact, I had to slow down for Caleb behind me.

I'd turn now and again to count the three other headlamps. How long was this culvert, anyway? I wondered if it ever got totally full of water, right to the ceiling. That would give the rats some ride. Maybe we should have started at the other end with inner tubes. The Wildmen would be impressed with that.

"Kip!" Caleb's voice sounded a little panicked.

"Yes?"

"How much farther?"

"How would I know?" I hoped we were more than halfway. My knees were killing me already. But I had to keep everyone moving. No way did we want to be here when the water got deeper. It was already getting hard to keep a handhold. Cold water lapped against my stomach. I shivered.

My hands hit something like a low wall. At the same time, I felt a rooster tail of water spraying my face. Yuck. Sewer-like water. I felt with my hands. A major pile of mud blocked the tunnel. Water flowed over it like a dam break. I sat on my haunches and directed my light on it.

"What's up?" I heard Fraser's voice from way behind. This time, there was no echo. The water swallowed our words now, like it was trying to swallow us.

"Mud blockage," I shouted. I thrust my head and shoulders over the top of the mud dam, hoping to squeeze through. All I earned for my efforts was a mouth full of foul-tasting water. My pulse began rising. We had to be near the end. No way was I going back. I punched at the little dirt dam. I began to claw at it. Then I remembered my cane. I pulled it from my backpack. I thrust it into the dam, where it stuck. Then I pulled it out. Again, and again. Finally the dam began falling apart under my attack. Water spat at me. It tried to sweep me off my knees as the mud pile collapsed. A mini mudslide. I thrust my hand forward and pulled myself beyond it.

"Eeeeahhhh," I said as one hand closed

over the carcass of something. A rat? A kitten? I pulled it up, saw the dangling black rat's tail and threw it as far ahead as I could.

As we rounded a corner, we struggled to keep the water from picking us up off our hands and knees. I felt Caleb's hand grip my pant leg. Was he checking that I was there or keeping himself from being pulled backward? I wished I had someone ahead to cling to. I was half swimming now, not easy with only one good leg.

"Almost there!" I shouted as I spotted a circle of daylight ahead. "Grab a foot," I shouted at Caleb, who'd slipped behind. "We're going to make it!" I swam-pulled-crawled.

Eventually, during a break between water surges, I splashed to within a few feet of the entrance. But I had a feeling the culvert gods were playing with us. I yanked my cane off my backpack again. This time I thrust it forward, reaching for the tunnel's sharp-edged rim. The cane's curved end caught the culvert's lip just as the next surge of water blasted full bore into my face. I held onto the end of my cane with a deadlock grip. It had to hold me and Caleb, who was clinging to my leg, and two other Daredevil Club members. We were a half-drowned human chain. I held my breath as long as I could.

The force of the water tore at me; my chest and shoulder muscles were stretched to the ripping point. But no way would I let go. When the surge ended, I thrust my upper body forward, exploded out of the culvert and grabbed for Caleb's arms. I kept contact even as I fell into the muddy pool beneath the waterfall that was feeding the culvert in surges.

"We made it," Caleb spluttered.

"Not till you pull Vlad out of there," I shouted. Caleb reached in and pulled on Vlad's wet, slippery arms. Vlad, in turn, did the same for Fraser.

We stood at the edge of the pool dripping and shivering. Rain pounded our heads even as it expanded the little falls that cascaded down the hill above the culvert.

"Number six was exciting!" Fraser said through chattering teeth. He peered back at the dark tunnel and shook himself like a dog. He smiled. "How'd you manage to hang on there at the end, Kip?"

I lifted my cane and demonstrated how I'd hooked it on the edge of the steel.

Fraser nodded soberly. He knew what the score would have been if I hadn't found an anchor hold.

"Good thing you went first," Vlad commented, studying my cane rather than my face as he said it.

"So," Caleb joked as he peeled off a layer of waterlogged clothing. "Do we climb back in and shoot down it like a waterslide?"

"*Not!*" we all chorused together.

I wondered if the drowned rat had shot out the other end yet.

## chapter five

The following Saturday, I made my way toward the bridge where I'd arranged to meet the other Daredevils. The bridge would be our number seven stunt. Although I'd suggested it, I was worried. It was forty feet above the lake, for one thing. Higher than a high diving board. Maybe not enough to kill us if we fell, but enough to do damage. I was an expert on falling into water and doing damage.

My other worry was how to pull myself

along the steel girders with a bad leg. It might pull me off center like an anchor ready to yank me into the water with every move. Not that I'd revealed any concerns to my teammates, of course.

Maybe scouting it would give me an answer. We'd agreed to meet at two. I'd decided to get there an hour early. As I was rounding a street corner, I was so busy thinking about how to tackle the girders that I smacked right into Dwayne Harvey. Dwayne was the tallest of the three Wildmen. He was solid with bushy uncombed red hair. He was the group's leader, a scary thought till you imagine either of his two buddies as leader. Dwayne might be kind of stupid and stubborn, but at least he was a mass of muscle. Roy and Dexter were lightweights and were totally out of shape.

"Well, well, taking a stroll through Peever, are we?" Dwayne asked me. His eyes ran up and down me, then up and down my cane.

I shrugged and looked past him to Roy

and Dexter approaching. "Sure, like you," I said.

"Wouldn't be a stroll to a water tower, now, would it? Guess you and your buddies have done that. Sorry about beating you out on the grain elevator. It was a blast, you know."

"Whatever," I said, moving past him.

"And the culvert was what, your number six?" Dwayne's buddy Dexter sneered as he placed himself in front of me.

"Depends on who's counting," I suggested.

"Hey, the kid's a smart aleck!" Dexter screeched, pulling a pack of gum from his shirt pocket. "He sure didn't learn his lesson jumping off that cliff, either. Want some gum, smart aleck?"

"No thanks," I said, dodging him and moving as fast as my cane would allow.

"Wanna hear my one-legged-man joke?" Roy, between snapping his gum, called after me.

I was moving fast enough to put some distance between us. I wasn't afraid. They were losers, all talk. But there were three of them, and one of me. Or three-quarters of me, anyway.

"We're keeping an eye on you," Dwayne shouted, laughing. "We're watching you, Daredevil dude. We'll beat you, you know."

I took a roundabout route to the bridge in case they followed. I got there half an hour before the agreed meeting time. I slowed when I saw the three Daredevils hunched together. They were talking with faces so serious you'd think they were planning World War III. It wasn't like them to be early. I hesitated.

I saw them high-five each other and break up. They were moving toward the road when they saw me. They stopped in their tracks. Fraser looked defiant. Vlad studied his shoes. Caleb's face turned a rainbow of colors. No one greeted me.

I kept my voice steady and casual and my gait even as I moved up to them. "Hey guys. Good to get here early, eh? So, do we have a strategy?" *And is the strategy to ditch me?*

No one replied. I directed my gaze at Caleb, who was as easy to read as a kids' book. "Caleb, how's it going?"

Caleb looked from Fraser to Vlad, nervous-like.

"It's going just fine," Fraser finally replied, too loudly.

"Have you decided whether we need rope? That first beam is kind of inaccessible."

The boys' eyes moved back to the beams.

"We thought we could take turns lifting each other to grab that first beam," Caleb said, all in a rush.

"But then what about the fourth person? How're we going to get the last one up without rope? Anyway, you see that big gap farther along the beam? What's our strategy for that?"

I used the words "we" and "our" with emphasis.

Fraser looked uncomfortable and moved toward the undersides of the bridge. He walked until he was right beneath the gap. It looked as if the bridge engineers had planned a way to foil anyone looking to climb along the girders. I could see that Fraser hadn't noticed how large the gap was. He stood there measuring it with his eyes.

"You guys said it'd be easy to get up to the beam," Caleb said accusingly. "You said we didn't need rope. And you didn't say anything about that gap."

Fraser just kept staring at the gap.

"It can't be done without rope," I said as authoritatively as I could.

"We agreed no rope," Fraser stated.

"Who cares if we use a little rope at the start? There's still a block and a half of bridge after the gap. Besides, have you checked out the other side? I bet there's the same funny gap in the beams there. Engineers like things symmetric. It can't be done without rope, Fraser."

He sucked in his breath. He didn't like being shown up. But he hadn't studied it carefully. Were they really planning to do it without a rope? And without me?

"Kip's right," Vlad ruled. "We can't

Tarzan across that gap without a rope. Let's say no rope except for the gaps at either end of the bridge."

"I agree!" Caleb said, his face flushed as he turned toward Fraser.

Fraser shrugged. "Yeah, okay. No biggie." He lifted his hand to high-five mine. "Saturday at ten, okay?"

"Saturday at ten," I agreed, relieved. *But maybe I'll get there at nine to be sure.*

As we moved away from the bridge, I glimpsed someone walking across it, eyes on us. Fearful it might be one of the Wildmen, I stopped for a better look. My eyes met Elyse's. She paused, hand on the leash of her German Shepherd. She hadn't heard our conversation; she was too far away. She was just out walking her dog. But as I turned away, I wished she hadn't seen us. She'd assume we were scouting for a stunt. She'd try to give me a hard time at the clinic. Well, let her. It was *my* life.

## chapter six

"Why do you always make a face when you come through the door?" Elyse asked me as the door slammed behind me. She was standing at the receptionist's desk, dusting the countertop.

"Maybe because those bells are off-tune," I replied, checking my watch. I hoped Andrew would get here soon. I didn't want to talk with Elyse Superior-to-Everyone Strauss.

She scratched her head. "How can jingle bells be out of tune?"

"Beats me, but they are." I flopped into a waiting-room seat. I reached for a motorcycle magazine. I opened to a two-page photo spread. It showed a guy on a dirt bike doing a backflip thirty feet above two piles of dirt. He'd used the first berm as a ramp to shoot up into the air. He planned to land on the sloping backside of the second. Frozen by the camera for that second, he was a daredevil hero. There was no way of knowing if things didn't work out. Maybe he miscalculated a fraction of a foot after the photographer snapped the picture. Maybe he fell like a rock and landed on his back. Maybe the bike fell on him. Maybe he's in a wheelchair now. Did he have regrets? No. A guy has to take chances, or life is boring. But maybe he had just a few secret regrets. Maybe he should've checked that bike more carefully before his run. Maybe he should've studied the landing longer.

I tossed the magazine onto the table. Most likely he was still doing backflips at freestyle events. He had tons of friends and fans, and was rich in prize money. And here I was, sitting in a physio clinic with a girl who'd never understand any of that.

"Want some coffee or tea?" she asked.

I wagged my head no. "You're taking this work-experience thing seriously, aren't you?"

Her eyebrows furrowed, and her nose lifted. "I take everything seriously. Not like some who only exist for a good time."

"You think coming here is a good time?" Even to me, my tone sounded venomous.

She looked startled, then lowered her eyes. "No, I only meant..."

"I know what you meant, and until you're a qualified physio, I'd rather you stick with dusting."

The bells jangled. "Good morning, Kip," Andrew said. He lacked his usual smile. "Right on time as always! And hello, Elyse. This place is looking as neat as a pin. What did we do before you started here?"

She beamed. I stood and shuffled toward the workout room.

"Kip, you're looking a little stiff today. What's going on?"

I waited until we were in the workout room. "Maybe I overdid it a little one day," I said, "but it's coming along, isn't it? How much longer?"

Andrew sighed and sat down. He looked at his shoes. He didn't even look up when Elyse slipped in.

"Kip, I have to be honest with you. You need at least two more months of physio. You'll never have your full range of movement back. We've already discussed that. But to maximize your recovery, you need to stick with a program..."

"I'm doing it, aren't I?" I felt panicked by his sad, distracted tone. He'd said himself I was his star patient.

"Yes, Kip, you've been my Olympian. But I have to tell you that one of this clinic's funding partners is pulling the plug. So we're short on rent. We may have to close. You're not going to get the last two months you need unless..."

"Unless what?" Elyse asked in an urgent tone.

"Unless we can raise a couple thousand

dollars to keep us going until we can get a new government grant."

"A couple thousand dollars?" Elyse's voice was full of dismay. "No one in Peever has that kind of money."

Andrew nodded. "I know. I only found out about the cuts earlier this week. I've lost a lot of sleep over it. I wish I could see a way, but I don't."

He sighed, stood, and forced a smile. "Enough of this. Sorry, kids. We still need to do what we're here to do. Elyse, the big rubber balls please. Kip, you said you overdid things the other day. Which muscles are hurting, and what brought that on?"

I saw Elyse's head turn my way. She had way too much interest in my reply.

"I'm fine. But could you draw me up a new program for something?"

"A new program?"

"To strengthen some muscles I don't normally use."

"To strengthen which muscles for what?" he asked, cocking his head and grabbing his clipboard.

"Well, I'm thinking of competing in a sort of goofy school athletic event. It requires me to wriggle along a raised bar like so." I straddled a nearby bench and mimicked how I intended to push myself along the girder on the bridge.

"You're joking or you're serious?" Andrew said with a broadening smile.

"Hey, I take everything I do seriously," I said, tossing a look at Elyse. "Even one-legged straddling contests."

"Well, now there's a category you should excel at," he said, laughing. "Believe it or not, I won a one-legged race back in junior high school, but it was upright with a partner. I won because I figured out how to train for it. So, what the heck, we can figure out a winning technique for that. Looks to me like you need to use your upper body more, your leg less."

He straddled the bench and kept launching himself forward on his palms, one placed atop the other, like someone leapfrogging. "This position would be much more efficient."

I smiled and got busy perfecting the new technique. When I snuck a look at Elyse, she rolled her eyes at me. She knew, or she thought she knew, but she wasn't going to say anything in front of Andrew. And I'd make sure she had no chance to offer her opinion before number seven was history.

## chapter seven

"Why Mud Lake?" I asked as Dad swung the car around a bend in the road. "There are three other lakes around Peever. We should try something different."

"Kip, dear," my mom replied, turning around from the front seat, "we haven't been back to Mud Lake since your accident."

"So? There are still three other lakes to choose from."

I had a suspicion about why they'd

51

chosen a family canoe trip here, and I didn't much like it.

"Kip, we can't keep going to the other lakes because you want to avoid Mud Lake."

"Who said I'm avoiding Mud Lake? It's just that the other three are bigger. And they have fewer mosquitoes," I added for good measure.

"Maybe so, but your father and I think it's time to visit Mud Lake again. Ever heard the expression, 'getting back on the horse'?"

"Getting back on the horse!" I spit the words out. "I can't believe you're saying that to me. I'm not scared of a stupid muddy lake. And I'm not scared of cliff-jumping or other daredevil stunts either," I finished loudly. I regretted the last line the minute it was out of my mouth. My mother's face flashed fright. So *that* was the real reason we were on our way to Mud Lake. They suspected I was still doing stunts, and thought a visit to the site of my accident might change my mind. Stupid parents. They think they're psychologists or something. Think they can outsmart me. They can't.

"Kip, it's just a family picnic. You don't have to canoe with us if you don't want to."

"You should have let me bring a friend," I groused.

"And what friend would you have chosen?" my mom asked.

I crossed my arms and sank lower into my seat. What did it matter who? But I wondered: Do I have any friends anymore? I replayed the bridge scene in my mind. The other Daredevils had met before our agreed time. They thought I'd take the hint, didn't they? Well, I wasn't going to. If I quit the Daredevil Club one stunt before the final one, what would everyone at school say? Who would I hang out with?

When Dad pulled into the parking lot, I was surprised to see half a dozen cars. Maybe there'd be other kids around. Even if there weren't, I could swim. Andrew had told me that swimming would be a great way to train for my "straddle school stunt." I eyed the dock on the other side of the small lake. Packed with kids. Bet I could make it there and back.

Either that, or I could head to the cliffs we'd jumped to prove a point to my parents. My head swiveled slowly toward the cliffs. They glinted in the sun: reddish rock with yellow and brown streaks. Picturesque cliffs innocently waiting for an unsuspecting victim. Waiting to play Russian roulette. Some townsfolk had voted to fence them off after my accident. More sensible people had said that it wouldn't stop anyone determined to jump from them. Kids had been jumping into Mud Lake from various places for generations. I wasn't the first to make contact with that underwater boulder. A girl had been killed here twenty years ago. Some said her ghost still lingered, that she screamed every time anyone stood too close to the edge of the cliffs. Had she heard me scream?

My eyes moved to the water below the cliffs. Of course you can't see the rock. You just have to know roughly where it is. Sometimes you can see its shadow lurking.

I closed my eyes. Pain shot up my left leg like fireworks. Like daggers trying to rip me up from the inside out. The whole day replayed in my mind, even though I tried to stop it. I pictured my feet shuffling to the cliff's edge. Me stepping off the cliff. The exhilarating fall. Whoops of encouragement from my audience. The frame I'd like to freeze and put in a double-page magazine spread, so I could halt or rewind the moment. The splash. The shock of the impact. The explosion of pain. The gasping, flailing, screaming. Fraser pulling me to safety. The ambulance.

The rest was history. With a bolt of anger, I realized my parents were reading my mind as we sat in the parking lot. I grabbed my cane and yanked on the car door handle. I let myself out and sucked in clean, fresh air.

"Go canoeing," I said. "I'm going to swim to the dock. I'll be back in an hour for lunch. Sound good?"

"Are you sure Andrew Pollack would approve that distance, Kip?" Dad asked.

"He said to swim as part of my training," I said. "I can always signal if I need you to pick me up in the canoe." In reality, Andrew would say that swimming to the dock and back was a little too far. But I figured no pain, no gain.

I poked my cane into the muddy beach like an explorer planting a flag. My parents off-loaded the canoe.

"Sure you don't want to canoe with us?" Dad asked.

"Maybe later," I said. "What's for lunch?"

"Chicken salad sandwiches, potato salad, carrots and brownies," Mom replied. "Your favorite brownies."

"Thanks! I'll swim hard for them," I promised cheerfully. I stripped to my swimming shorts and allowed Dad to help me to the water's edge. I stuck a toe in. Warm. Way warmer than the water that had almost drowned us in the culvert.

I slipped into the water and started toward the dock. I loved swimming. In water, I looked normal. No one could identify a handicap. In the water, my buff upper body almost made up for what Mud Lake had taken away.

Today, Mud Lake was warm, lapping, and I was Kip Fox, mighty swimmer. Star physio patient. If we managed to keep our physio, that is. Andrew's news was something I tried to keep out of my mind. I didn't want to lose my workouts, or work with anyone but Andrew. I didn't want to see him forced out of Peever.

Arm over arm, I stroked. I pretended I was an Olympic swimmer in training. Slow and steady, going for maximum distance. "If I get to the dock and back, I'll have no trouble with the bridge," I told myself.

Closer and closer came the dock. I could see people on it, and the diving board at one end. As I drew close, I saw little kids leaping, diving and laughing. One figure was bigger than the little kids. A girl sunbathing primly on a towel. She had parked herself as far from the board as she could to avoid splashes. She was scowling at the little kids having fun. Oh no. Not here. It couldn't be Elyse Strauss.

It was too late to turn around. Not only because she'd seen me, but because I was tired. I needed a rest on the dock before heading back. But wasn't this just my rotten luck?

She sat up and crossed her arms and legs. "Kip Fox. Did Mr. Pollack give you permission to swim *all* the way across the lake? I heard him say no more than fifteen minutes of swimming a day. You are overdoing it, and I'm not jumping in to save you if you have problems."

"Elyse Strauss, did anyone ask you to save anyone? You look afraid of getting wet."

I heaved myself up onto the dock in one swift move. Sounds like no big deal, but it had taken me a lot of bench-pressing to accomplish that. I turned my back on Elyse and staked out a place in the sun. I recognized two kids on the dock, neighbors. Little kids, maybe six years old.

"Hey, Harry, bet you can't do a cannonball. Hey, Sharon, show me a dive."

"I can do a cannonball! I can dive! Watch *me*!" a chorus of young voices begged all at once.

"Okay, one at a time."

Seconds later, I shouted, "Nice one, Harry. A nine out of ten. And Sharon, I'll give you an eight. Who can beat them? Who's next?"

The kids loved it. Soon they were bouncing all over me, trying to tickle me and push me in. It gave me something to do and allowed me to ignore Elyse.

Pretty soon I'd had enough of the kids, and my stomach was rumbling with hunger. "Okay, who wants to see a real cannonball?" I shouted.

"I do! I do!" They jumped up and down, giggling.

Elyse sat up, clearly alarmed at the thought of getting splashed even worse. She pulled her towel around her.

"See you around, kids!" I shouted. "Later, cleaning lady!"

I used my half-recovered leg muscles to put a real bounce in that board before

I shot up high. I curled into an untidy ball—the best I could with the bad leg—and came down hard. When I surfaced, the kids cheered like mad. Elyse's hair clung in clumps around her frowning face. Her waterlogged towel had fallen off.

I waved and swam like the athlete I am. I made it all the way back to the brownies, no problem. A feat to report to Andrew, preferably in front of his work-experience student.

# chapter eight

Saturday dawned bright and warm, yet I awoke nervous.

"Snap out of it," I told myself. "It's a perfect day, and this is the last stunt. We'll be celebrating tonight."

Still, as I headed toward the bridge, I couldn't relax my face muscles or loosen my shoulders. Ever since my accident, I've been able to tell how a day is going to go the minute I wake up. At the start of a good day, my left leg feels tingly, like it's full of electricity. I get a bad-day warning when I feel a dull pain pulsing up and down it. Andrew told me that my left limb lost lots of nerve endings. But I swear that when it lost its job of helping me walk, my leg decided to try out for a new position: psychic. I'd learned to listen to my leg. This morning, I'd listened hard. But strangely, there'd been no sensation at all. It refused to tell me how things were going to turn out. Like it had turned in its psychic badge.

I reached the bridge at nine o'clock. The only sign of life was a couple of grizzled-looking homeless people. They were asleep in tattered sleeping bags. I shook my head. Even Peever had homeless people? I guessed the bridge protected them from rain and wind on less glorious days. I looked up. Crows flapped their wings and rested on supports high above us, peering down like gargoyles.

I paused upwind of the vagrants' smelly camp. I sat and stared at the ironwork above. *Way* above. If two guys stood on one another's shoulders, they could reach the beams under the bridge where it starts. But the ground drops rapidly away where the gravel bank runs down to the lake. By the time the bridge is over the water, the beams beneath it are almost forty feet up. That would be like looking down from the roof of a four-story building. Falling into the water from there could be seriously bruising.

I focused on the long steel beams that ran horizontally beneath V-shaped supports. The beams vibrated a little each time trucks passed over. Straddle the beam, I told myself, and place your hands in front of you. Like a cowboy on the horn of his saddle. Lean forward, weight on your hands, lift the buttocks, and keep shuffling. No swaying, 'cause the second you go off-center, you have no power to stop a fall.

Maintaining balance when your hands are busy requires two legs. I'd have to make do with one. I looked out to the water. I studied it closely. My breath ran out of me; my chest tightened. There was a shadow—a hidden boulder lay twenty yards offshore. Directly under the beam. No falling off there.

We'll have it dialed by then, I told myself.

Shouts, whistles, and laughter broke my concentration. I turned around and frowned. Three Wildmen were approaching. Quickly I stepped behind a bridge pillar. They drew up beside the vagrants, pointing and guffawing. Then they started tossing small stones at the still figures. That got the bums stirring real fast.

"Hey, wakey wakey, boys. We come to give you a show!" said Dexter. "Hey, dudes!" Roy shouted.

"Whatcha doin', man?" a bum shouted at him, wiping his face.

"We're here to give you guys a show!" Dexter responded. "Looky the beams up there. We're gonna climb up there. Betchya never saw anythin' like that! Wake up and see the show, dudes!" He kicked one figure after another, until all the bums were sitting up. They blinked in the morning light.

Dwayne, wearing a small backpack, reached the beam with a lift from his buddies. Next, Roy wavered atop Dexter's shoulders as Dwayne reached down to help him up. Dexter recruited two of the homeless guys to hoist him up.

With lots of whooping and hollering, the Wildmen straddled and moved along the beams. Beneath them, the gravel bank dropped away steeply. No one had spotted me yet. I looked frantically behind me for a sign of approaching Daredevils. The Wildmen were attempting to beat us right in front of my eyes. The Daredevils should've planned to meet earlier!

Dwayne reached the gap and busied himself tying his rope to the beam. He'll make it, I thought, but the other guys aren't strong enough.

I looked at the rocky bank two stories under the gap. The bank's steepness let up for a few feet, forming a bench of small, sharp rocks before it continued to plunge to the water. I could picture these guys falling twenty feet onto that ledge of rocks. Then maybe rolling off it and continuing to the water. That would be bad. Very bad. Someone was going to get hurt. I didn't need a psychic leg to tell me that. The bridge bums were up and milling about now. They were shading their eyes with their hands as they stared up, openmouthed, at the Wildmen. I sprang out from behind my pillar and grabbed their ratty sleeping bags.

"Guys, I'm just borrowing these for a minute," I told the bums. I ran and dumped the bags onto the ledge under the gap. It wasn't a trampoline or anything, but it made me feel a little better. Stupid Wildmen.

"Hey, whatcha doin' with our bags?" the bums demanded, but they didn't move to grab me or anything.

Dwayne spotted me. "Kip! Hey, guys, if it ain't a Daredevil. All on his lonesome, come for the show. And stealin' the bums' stuff too."

"Dwayne, call it off. You guys are going to get hurt."

"Kip, whose side are you on?" an angry voice sounded behind me. I whirled around to see Fraser.

"Hey, Wildmen!" Dwayne shouted to his buddies. "We got the full Daredevil team now for spectators. So sorry, guys, but we beat you to it! See ya on the other side," he called down to Fraser and me as Vlad and Caleb joined us. He tested the rope with a little tug and winked at me.

"Fraser," I said quietly, my eyes not leaving Dwayne. "I got here as they were climbing. Roy and Dexter aren't fit enough to make it across that gap. They're going to get hurt."

"They're idiots," Vlad agreed. "They won't make it."

"Yeah," Fraser added. "It doesn't count unless they all make it. We can start up there after someone falls and Dwayne gives in."

Caleb just stood there, mouth slightly open. I was struck dumb myself. Fraser and Vlad didn't care if someone got hurt? We watched Dwayne swing like a gorilla on the rope. He wrapped his big hands around the next beam, and pulled himself up with pumped biceps. The guy was built like a linebacker. He yahooed and swung the rope back to his buddies.

"All right!" Roy shouted as he took the rope in hand.

"Roy, don't do it," I called up.

My team—Fraser, Vlad, and Caleb—turned to stare at me. Roy broke into high-pitched laughter, locked eyes with me, and swung. His head nearly slammed into the far beam. He groped for a hold. Then his eyes grew wide, and he dropped like a gunshot bird. He landed in the pile of smelly sleeping bags and began rolling down the bank. Luckily, he stopped before the water. He sat up holding his head, which was bleeding. His lower legs were cut up too. Without the cushion I'd provided, he'd have gotten way worse than a few cuts.

I scrambled down and saw that he was only stunned. Puffing as I jabbed my cane into the loose gravel slope, I returned with the scattered sleeping bags. I put them back into place under the gap. I moved away barely in time to miss being hit by a second falling body. Dexter sprang up and kicked the bank angrily. He shook a fist at me. "It's your fault!" he bellowed. "You distracted us!"

I shook my head. Like I hadn't just saved him from near death.

Higher up the bank, the bums the Wildmen had woken up were clapping and cheering. I looked up to see Dwayne shaking his head sadly side to side. Under the bridge Fraser and Vlad were kicking rocks and dust in my direction. What for? My sleeping-bag interference? Caleb was backing away.

"Traitor," Fraser and Vlad yelled.

"Keep going!" the bums were shouting up to Dwayne now. But he was setting up a second rope to swing back on. "Chicken!" they screeched and started picking up rocks to throw at Dwayne.

"Hey!" Dexter said and aimed some rocks at the bums.

"The guy up there has to get down!" I tried telling the bums, ignoring the glares from my own teammates. Next thing I knew, the homeless guys' rocks were whistling past my ears, and my teammates had vanished.

That's when the sirens sounded.

"Cops!" everyone yelled. You never saw so many bodies scattering.

My cane went into action pretty fast. I was out of sight and just innocently sauntering along by the time the squad cars pulled up. I glanced back to see Dwayne touch ground and outrun an officer.

As the other police poked about the site, the realization hit me: I'd just made enemies of both the Wildmen and the Daredevils.

# chapter nine

I learned how much damage I'd done when I stepped into the Cowboy Café half an hour later. Fraser, Vlad and Caleb were there. Fraser and Vlad glared at me and left abruptly. That left Caleb sitting there, hands in his lap.

I plunked down beside him. "Well, we didn't get caught," I said.

"Kip," Caleb began, "there's something I've been wanting to tell you."

"Then tell me," I said, hanging my cane over the straight back of our plastic booth.

"I'm thinking of dropping out of the Daredevils."

"Are you, now?" I said, not believing him for a second.

"And Kip, I think you should too. It's dumb. Not just 'cause we're going to get caught, but 'cause someone is going to get hurt. Hurt *again*," he added.

"Fraser and Vlad put you up to this, didn't they?" I asked.

"No! Kip, they didn't! Honest, I've wanted to quit for a while. I can't believe you're still into this stuff after your accident. Each stunt has gotten riskier. Don't you think?"

"That was the plan from the start. Remember who came up with the list of stunts?"

He nodded.

"Who put you up to this, Caleb? I started the dares, and I'm going to finish them. Quit if you like, but I'm not."

"Kip..."

"Tell Fraser and Vlad I'm not having it. If they want to tell me where to go, they have to do it to my face, not through you."

I stood up and turned my back on him.

"Liar!" I shouted and walked out. My heart pounded against my chest. I wouldn't normally talk to Caleb like that, but no one was telling me when to quit.

I decided to walk off my anger. I walked straight down Main Street, my cane working the hot pavement. I walked till both my legs were aching. When I looked for somewhere to rest, I found myself in front of the physio clinic.

A breeze had picked up. It was ruffling a piece of paper taped to the door. I shuffled over for a look.

"Reduced hours," it read. I tried the door. Locked. The clinic should've opened an hour ago. Where was Andrew? I read the small type on the notice. Something about funding cuts and temporarily reduced hours.

"Just great!" I shouted, kicking the door. No Andrew, no finishing what I'd worked so hard to achieve. All because of some lousy funding partner. I kicked the door again.

"Hey, you'll make those off-tune bells sound," a voice stated.

I turned around. Elyse, of course. I'd have said something sarcastic, but her face looked pretty long too. I sat down on the steps. She plunked down beside me.

"I've lost my work-study hours," she said. "And you're going to lose your physio. There are lots of other patients who depend on Andrew too. Pretty rotten, huh?"

"I didn't expect it to happen so fast," I admitted.

"You know," she said, "I think we should help Andrew."

"Help Andrew?"

"Well, I've done fundraising for school events. It's not that hard. Andrew said we only need two months' rent to keep things going till a government grant can help."

"Oh sure," I said bitterly. "You bake cookies. I'll run the one-legged race."

Elyse looked at me, but for once, she didn't take the bait. "Hey, that's it, Kip. A carnival. The whole town would get behind it."

"A carnival?" I said. "What kind of carnival? Apple bobbing, ring tossing, bingo?" I laughed, trying to picture such a thing on Peever's Main Street. "Hey, maybe my gang could do the stunts," I said, laying on the sarcasm. "No doubt Peeverites would pay big to watch us bungee jump off the City Hall clock..."

"Kip, I didn't say anything about stunts, but you gave me an idea. A street carnival would work! Yes, apple bobbing and bingo would bring people. You could help with booths like that. You're good with little kids. You could even come up with some high-action thing that little kids will think is cool. A soapbox derby race on Hill Street or something. People would pay for their kids to do that."

"You've lost your mind, Elyse. I do stunts for myself. I don't coordinate kiddie games."

"You did at the dock that day. And this isn't about stunts, Kip. We're talking a family street carnival. You're from the city. You wouldn't know. Small towns like ours do fundraising carnivals. Really! You and I could raise the money for the clinic's rent if everyone got behind it. Maybe the Wildmen and your weird friends could pitch in."

"Weird friends?"

"Well, what you guys do for kicks isn't very normal."

"What would you know about normal?"

"Kip, for once, let's not fight. We both want the clinic to stay open, don't we?"

The girl was a little odd, but she was persuasive too. And she was right about me wanting Andrew to stay. I tried to imagine what Fraser and Vlad would say about running a soapbox derby: pushing pedal cars over a start line at the top of a hill as kids screamed with excitement. Fraser and Vlad both had a pack of little brothers and sisters at home. They did stuff like that all the time. They might help out, just for the kick of it. I'd even try Dwayne, Roy and Dexter.

I turned and smiled at Elyse. "Okay, maybe you're onto something. I'll talk with the gang. No promises."

"I don't need promises. I know you'll do it. You started up the Daredevils. Leaders make things happen," she said.

## chapter ten

At Cowboy Café, I ordered a double cheeseburger, onion rings and chocolate milkshake. Elyse ordered a diet cola and fries.

"Fries are potatoes, which are vegetables," she said with a half smile.

I allowed myself to smile, something I hadn't done much of in a while. I'd decided Elyse wasn't all bad. She just needed someone to help her lighten up.

We sat huddled over our notebook of carnival booth ideas, glancing up at the door every few seconds. We were expecting the Daredevils and Andrew.

The Daredevils arrived a little late. They ordered food before sauntering over to our booth. Fraser glared at Elyse before taking a seat near me. Vlad took up the entire next booth and put his feet up on the table. Caleb smiled at Elyse hesitantly, then seated himself opposite Vlad.

"Hi guys, thanks for coming," I started. "This is Elyse Strauss, as you know. She's coordinating the carnival. But you guys get to help me plan some stuff."

"Have the Wildmen agreed to be at this carnival?" Fraser asked curtly.

"Of course not," I said. I'd tried, as if I had a hope with those losers.

"Whose stupid idea was this?" Vlad demanded.

"Mine," I said before Elyse could answer. "I need two more months of physio to mend. I lose my physio if we don't do this. You guys can join us to help my recovery.

Or to prove that the Daredevils do more than stunts on the sneak. But just do it, okay?"

My stern voice surprised me. A leader's voice, like before my accident.

"What's on your list?" Fraser demanded.

I handed him the notebook and a pencil. "We've outlined a few things. Add any others you'd like. The hardware store has offered to provide whatever we need to build booths."

Vlad sat up, grabbed the notebook from Fraser, read it, and looked at me. "Seriously? These are totally boring. I have a better idea. I was at a carnival once that had a dunk tank. People paid to get friends soaking wet. I could build one of those."

"Perfect. Make a list of what you need. The hardware store will hand it over."

Fraser's hand came over the booth partition to punch Vlad in the shoulder. "You do that. I'll wave the flag at the bottom of the soapbox derby race."

I looked at Caleb.

"How about I help with safety at the

soapbox derby?" he said, dipping a plastic spoon into his strawberry sundae.

"Well, that's great," I said, elated. Just then, Andrew entered, walked over, and laid a hand on my shoulder.

"Kip! Elyse! And these must be your friends."

I introduced Andrew around. Fraser and Vlad eyed him warily. Caleb stood to shake his hand.

"Guys, I can't tell you how much I appreciate your efforts," Andrew said. "Not just Kip, but a dozen folks in Peever rely on the clinic. If it gets shut down, a lot of them will suffer. Not to mention that you fellows never know when you might need my services." He winked at the group. "So you're doing a great thing."

The guys shifted their feet like they'd forgotten what this was really about.

"So, let's see the list." Someone handed him the notebook. He scanned it and smiled. "I'm good with everything you've come up with so far. Brainstorm some more if you like."

By the end of our meeting, we'd consumed lots of Cowboy Café food and enjoyed some good laughs. We'd added a few suggestions to the list. We'd even convinced Andrew to get his band to perform. I was feeling pretty good as everyone shook hands and headed for the door. When I noticed Elyse hanging back, I waited to walk out with her.

"Kip, there's something I want to tell you."

"Go for it." We crossed the parking lot and started up the street.

"Caleb is quitting the Daredevils. He told me yesterday. Has he told you?"

I remembered our last conversation. I'd accused him of pretending to try to get me to quit. But Caleb wouldn't play games with Elyse. Maybe I'd been too quick to decide he was lying.

"Well, he hasn't quit yet. And he's going to help out at the carnival."

"The carnival, yes. But the bridge, no."

So Elyse knew about the bridge. I slowed my steps.

"It's your decision, Kip, but I hope you'll also decide not to do the bridge." Her eyes were steady. Before I could reply, she added, "Kip, if Fraser and Vlad are trying to ditch you, they're not real friends. It's not worth re-injuring yourself to stay in with people like that."

Heat flared in my cheeks. My cane had half a mind to push Elyse away. Caleb had no right to tell her what was going on. She had no right to stick her nose into it. But the momentary flash of anger fizzled out. A bitter taste filled my mouth. I swallowed, but it remained.

"Caleb really isn't doing the bridge? *He* made that decision?" I asked.

"He decided. He thinks it's too dangerous. Plus, he's worried about his former leader."

*Former* leader. We'll see about that, I thought. I had to mull over her news.

"Well, thanks for telling me. See you later, Elyse. Good work on the carnival."

"I wouldn't have pulled it together without your help, Kip. People look up to you, you know. More people than you think."

"Maybe," I mumbled. I felt drained of all energy as I limped home.

# chapter eleven

Two days after the carnival meeting, Fraser, Vlad and I still hadn't planned a date for the bridge climb. We had to do it soon, or the Wildmen would do it. The urgency of the situation made me restless. Neither Fraser nor Vlad were returning my phone calls, and I couldn't leave messages their parents might interpret. So I decided to walk through town to find them.

As I walked, Elyse's words kept playing

themselves on an unwanted loop through my head. "If Fraser and Vlad are trying to ditch you, they're not real friends. It's not worth re-injuring yourself to stay in with people like that."

Well, she might be wrong. Anyway, I had no backup friends. And it was my decision to take risks. I wasn't like Caleb. I wasn't scared. I wasn't a quitter. I was within sight of the Cowboy Café when I spotted Fraser and Vlad. Some tall guy was with them. I couldn't make out who, but it wasn't Caleb.

They glanced behind them once but didn't see me. I decided to follow. I almost lost them. It's tough to keep up with three strong guys when you're using a cane. But when I judged them to be heading for the bridge, I doubled my efforts.

My breath caught as I drew close enough to recognize the third guy: Dwayne. My mind started racing. Had Dwayne finally tired of his two sidekicks? Had Fraser and Vlad replaced Caleb and me with Dwayne? Anger began to work its way from my gut to my chest. Soon I was panting and sweating—on fire with rage. You don't dump a teammate for a brainless goon right before the last stunt. It wasn't fair. It seemed too dirty a trick for Fraser and Vlad.

As they reached the bridge, I circled around so I'd be within earshot but not sight. I crouched down and rested, my hands shaking. I'd climb with them, whether they were planning it or not. That would show them.

Show them what? I thought. Is it worth re-injuring yourself? My jaw loosened. Where had that come from? I stuffed my cane into the dirt to help me stand up, but their conversation caused me to sink back out of sight.

"...never was cut out for it," Fraser was saying.

"...better off without him," Vlad added.

I felt my blood begin to boil. I edged closer.

"Okay guy, though," Dwayne said as Fraser unloaded rope from his pack. I couldn't see anyone's face, only their fingers working together to untangle the rope. "And you gotta give 'im points for volunteerin' to quit the Daredevils when he figured out it wasn't for him."

So they were talking about Caleb, not me!

"He was okay till the stunts got harder," Fraser said, tossing a rock down the bank toward the water. "He'd have quit sooner but he wanted to keep an eye on Kip."

"Kip's gonna be majorly ticked when he finds out we did this without him," Dwayne offered.

You've got that right, you jerk, I thought.

"Yeah, well he wouldn't listen to Caleb." It was Fraser's voice. "He's the most go-for-it of all of us. That's his real problem, not the leg."

What was that supposed to mean?

"Maybe we shoulda told him straight out," Vlad said.

"How can you tell a hard-core guy like Kip he's going to hurt himself?" Fraser demanded. "You can't just say, 'Hey dude, we know you'll keep going right to the end. We're totally amazed at your guts. But it ain't right, lettin' you do stuff that's gonna get you hurt again.'"

"That's a speech he wouldn't listen to," Dwayne agreed.

Vlad took a turn. "Maybe we shoulda said, 'Kip, your list was awesome. It *is* still awesome. But it was made before your accident. This stuff needs two legs. Number seven does, anyway. We want to finish the dares without seeing you hurt again.'" There was silence. I watched three rocks slung into the water. I wiped sweat off my forehead.

"We shoulda said something like that instead of sneaking here," Fraser finished.

"You'll explain it after. Now that you've sorta practiced," Dwayne suggested lamely. "Or Caleb will tell 'im."

I sat stock-still. I felt frozen to the ground. Then I heard the rope tossed over the beam. This was when I'd planned to step out and let them know I was here.

But I couldn't move. And not 'cause of what they'd just said. A powerhouse of pain racked my left leg. I gripped it with my hands as my head turned itself toward the lake to stare at the underwater rock. Its shadow seemed to darken and widen like a pool of blood. My breath caught.

"Well, here's to Kip," I heard Vlad announce. I saw one of his arms lift his water bottle. "We dedicate the final stunt to our true leader, who we had to protect from himself," he added in a dramatic tone.

Huh? I was busy hugging my leg to my chest, trying to massage the demons out of it. *Someone was going to get hurt.*

When I peeked out from behind my pillar, I saw they'd managed to get themselves up on the beam. By the time I'd staggered out in full view, they were shimmying toward the gap at high speed. Three guys, all strong and fit, Fraser leading. It wasn't like last time, I reminded myself. There was no nervous Caleb, no lightweight Wildmen. No one pretending he had two good legs. They stood a good chance of making it.

But my leg told me otherwise.

"Guys," I called up.

They looked down and froze for a second. I read shock and guilt.

"Kip..." they began.

"Forget about me. I'm okay with you guys going without me." For the first time, I really was. I'd have fallen somewhere along the way. One leg wasn't good enough here. I finally knew that. I'd have re-injured, like the guys said. Why could I admit that now?

People look up to you, you know. More people than you think.

"But guys, you need to use the rope over the boulder, okay?"

Fraser's face darkened. "No, we agreed no rope after the gap."

"Fraser, trust me. You need it, okay?" I wasn't sure which one needed it. My psychic leg wasn't that specific.

"We'll see," Fraser mumbled. He sat there as if needing to mull it over.

"No way!" declared Dwayne. He clambered over Fraser, grabbed the rope, and swung across the gap. Anger surged in me. Dwayne had used Fraser's hesitation to grab the lead. Dwayne made it, of course. He perched there, smiled at me, and swung the rope back to his new teammates.

Fraser and Vlad nodded at me and took their turns. Both made the gap. I let out a long sigh. But it wasn't the gap that worried me today. I watched Fraser stuff the rope into his pack as his teammates moved forward. They were doing the gentle leapfrogging movement Andrew and I had worked out. The difference was, every now and again they'd press their knees or heels against the steel beam like horse riders applying spurs. Just a little pressure to maintain balance. A pressure I couldn't have counted on.

They wriggled forward like three monkeys: Dwayne, Fraser and Vlad. They paused as they got out over the water. They turned and waved at me.

"The rope," I reminded them, but Dwayne shook his head firmly "no." Idiot.

Every second took them farther away.

They were out of earshot now, wriggling ever closer to that shadow waiting like a crocodile below. Fraser paused and opened his pack. He's going to take my advice! I thought. He's going to make everyone use the rope. But Dwayne moved his powerful shoulders and haunches ahead. Fraser called to him. Dwayne shook his head.

Fraser sat there watching him, rope in hand. My heart sank. My throat constricted. My leg's pulse overpowered my heartbeat as Dwayne moved over the danger zone. I closed my eyes. I tried not to see my own accident in slow motion. Tried not to feel my leg shatter on the rock.

When I opened my eyes, Dwayne was past the boulder, chugging along like a kid on an amusement-park mini-train. The guy had powerful haunches. He'd make it all the way. I was so busy watching him, I barely saw Fraser turn behind him to pass his backpack to Vlad.

"Dwayne did it without rope, so I can." I could read Fraser's mind. "We agreed no rope after the gap."

I broke into a sweat. I watched Fraser work the steel beam like he was riding a horse at a canter. But midway through one of Fraser's lifts, it was as if a spur broke, or a saddle slipped. I saw his body waver, his hands grab at the air. He fell away from the beam. His cry made Dwayne turn. I didn't see Fraser hit the water, because I was too busy slipping and sliding down the steep riverbank. I threw my cane away, sent my shoes flying, and leapt in. The water's chill sucked my breath out of me, but I'd hardly surfaced before I began pumping my arms. Hand over hand. One leg kicking. All my strength applied itself to reaching his flailing body.

"Fraser!" I shouted. I remembered to grab him from behind his head and speak calming words. I crooked my elbow loosely under his chin in the lifeguard's rescue position. I looked up and saw Vlad turning and heading back. I splashed toward shore towing my friend. Yes, he was my friend, I reminded myself. Vlad moved swiftly along the bridge beam in the same direction, high overhead. Dwayne looked back and shrugged, then kept moving forward. He was an engine who'd lost his cars. But that wasn't going to stop him from trying to reach his destination. He was a total, 100 percent jerk.

"I'm hurt. I'm hurt," Fraser was saying through clenched teeth.

"I know," I said. I hoped he'd injured himself far less than I had. I kicked madly with my good leg and free arm. Was I imagining it, or was my left leg putting out some power too? It was calling on memory: the memory of what it used to do, and the memory of when its shattered self was being towed by Fraser months earlier.

"Relax," I whispered. "You're going to be okay."

# chapter twelve

"Go! Go! Go!" I pushed the little wooden pedal car over the starting line. I let go and cheered the little kid. I imagined the feel of the air whistling past his ears and the adrenalin coursing through his short chubby arms as he gripped the steering wheel. The car headed too far right. The kid leaned left. Way left. More left. Oops, too far left. His wooden car hit the hay bale, spun, and skidded to a halt. Caleb leapt up onto the hay bale. He lifted the kid out and the crowd erupted into cheers. The little freckled face broke into a wide grin as his feet touched the ground and his proud dad came running.

I looked down the hill to the finish line. Fraser, leaning on his new cane, was waving the black and white checkered flag like a madman as a car crossed the finish line. Then he stuck a whistle in his mouth and sounded a shrill warning as two more cars careened down the hill and banged into one another. Caleb jumped over the hay bales again, lifting kids and wooden cars out of harm's way.

It was nice of the local farmers to donate all those hay bales, I thought, and nice of a local carpenter to repair the old pedal cars that had been sitting in someone's barn for a while. Living in a rural town wasn't so bad after all. The whole community had pulled together for the event. The steady number of coins dropping into the cans that Elyse and her crew carried created a musical jangle.

After the last car had run, I hobbled down to the finish line and clapped Fraser on the back. I pointed at his cane.

"Stupid-looking thing," I pronounced. He'd wound and glued a long rubber snake, complete with forked red tongue, around it.

"Better than your boring cane," Fraser retorted, making a face.

He'd only grazed the underwater boulder under the bridge that day. It had seriously bruised his hip.

"You two'll finish mending around the same time," Andrew had predicted. "Good thing I'm still in town, eh?"

"Hey! It's the derby starter and finish flagman standing together," the local newspaper photographer said. "Can I get a photo?"

Fraser and I leaned toward each other and smiled, our canes behind our backs.

"What's next?" I asked.

"Vlad's operating the dunk tank," Fraser said, swinging his cane forward to start up the hill.

We filed up Hill Street and turned onto Main to the sounds of rock music: Andrew's band. They weren't bad. We stopped to check out Vlad's creation. The dunk tank was a collapsing seat over a tank of water. A willing victim would climb up and sit on the seat. Then people who paid five dollars could toss balls at the device that would make the seat collapse and drop their friend into the tank.

Elyse hovered nearby collecting money in a can, her eyes dancing.

"How much has this pulled in?" I asked her, glancing around at the other stands. There were kids trying to dunk balls through basketball hoops, kids trying to land rings around bottles, and stuff like that. My dad was throwing darts, trying to win my mom a stuffed giraffe. How embarrassing.

"This is the biggest money maker of them all," Elyse said proudly. There've been lineups all day."

"Have you had a dunk yet?" I asked Elyse.

She giggled. "No, I'm not one of the

volunteers for that. Not that you're the first to ask."

"Hand me your money bucket for a moment."

She looked at me quizzically but handed it over.

"Hey everybody," I shouted into a crowd of kids our age. "Who'd pay a hundred bucks to see Elyse dunked?"

They stared at me, and at Elyse's widening eyes.

Then they all surged forward, digging coins out of their pockets.

"But Kip, you can't do this. I haven't volunteered..."

"Hey, here's a twenty," Fraser said, tossing a dirty, torn bill into the can. He grinned at Elyse. "I hear you serve drinks and fetch balls at Andrew's clinic."

"I'm in for fifteen," Vlad added.

"Hey everyone, just thirty more dollars, and Elyse is all wet!"

Laughter, smiles, and more coins clinking.

"I'd start climbing the dunk-tank ladder if I were you, Elyse," I teased.

A smile tugged at her lips. She threw me a mock glower and took off her shoes. She moved to the ladder.

"Elyse! Elyse! Elyse!" the crowd chanted. "Hundred-dollar Elyse!"

She sat primly on the seat and tucked her T-shirt into her shorts. She pinched her fingers over her nose. She gave me a brave salute and waited. I gathered up an armful of balls and started throwing.

"Go, Kip! Go, Kip!" the crowd yelled.

Elyse's shoulders hunched. I remembered her shivering on the dock after my cannonball. She'd loosened up since then. Not a lot, but there was hope. And people were being nicer to her since she'd organized this event. Me especially, if you didn't count this move.

I drew my arm back and threw. Bull's-eye. The chair collapsed. The girl dropped. Water sloshed up and over the tank sides. Fraser and I lifted our canes and crossed them like swords at a ceremony. Vlad and Caleb shouted "Yes!" On stage, Andrew paused to throw back his head and laugh.

The crowd clapped as she climbed out like a wet rat: a smiling wet rat.

"Fifty for Kip!" Andrew suddenly shouted.

"Fifty for Andrew!" I countered.

"A hundred for both!" someone else yelled.

It went on all afternoon. Fun, games and money. I got dunked more than once. I never realized how many "friends" I had in Peever. At the end of the day, as I stood taking it all in, Elyse and Andrew approached. They were holding trays of money cans collected from the volunteers.

"Guess how much?" Elyse, who'd changed into dry clothing, asked. She looked so pleased I thought she'd start jumping up and down.

"Enough?" I asked, looking to Andrew.

"Plenty enough," he said, clamping one hand on my shoulder, and one on Elyse's. "We're good for at least a few more months. That includes you, Fraser." He winked at his newest patient. Then his face turned stern. "Don't any of you think that helping out today means you can slack off at the clinic. In fact, I'm not sure you are up to the tough new program I've drawn up."

"You think not?" Fraser said, raising an eyebrow.

I smiled. "Is that a dare?"

**Pam Withers** wrote *Daredevil Club* after a back injury. During her recovery, she missed being able to participate in sports activities with her friends and family, and she started to wonder what would happen if someone were so set on keeping up with their pre-injury activities that they took unreasonable risks. Pam is the best-selling author of several sports adventure novels for young people, including *Camp Wild* and *Breathless*. Pam lives in Vancouver, British Columbia.